Play-along for
TODAY'S
SHOWSTOPPERS!

Published by
Wise Publications
14 -15 Berners Street, London W1T 3LJ, UK.

Exclusive Distributors:
Music Sales Limited
Distribution Centre, Newmarket Road, Bury St Edmunds,
Suffolk IP33 3YB, UK.
Music Sales Pty Limited
120 Rothschild Avenue, Rosebery, NSW 2018, Australia.

Order No. AM1001473
ISBN 13: 978-1-84938-674-6
This book © Copyright 2010 Wise Publications,
a division of Music Sales Limited.

Top line arrangements by Chris Hussey.
Engraving supplied by Camden Music.
Backing tracks by John Maul,
except 'Suddenly Seymour' by Danny Gluckstein.
Edited by Lizzie Moore.

CD recorded, mixed and mastered by Jonas Persson.
Flute played by Howard McGill.

Printed in the EU.

Guest Spot

Play-along for Flute

TODAY'S
SHOWSTOPPERS!

Wise Publications
part of The Music Sales Group
LONDON / NEW YORK / PARIS / SYDNEY / COPENHAGEN / BERLIN / MADRID / HONG KONG / TOKYO

Flute Fingering Chart

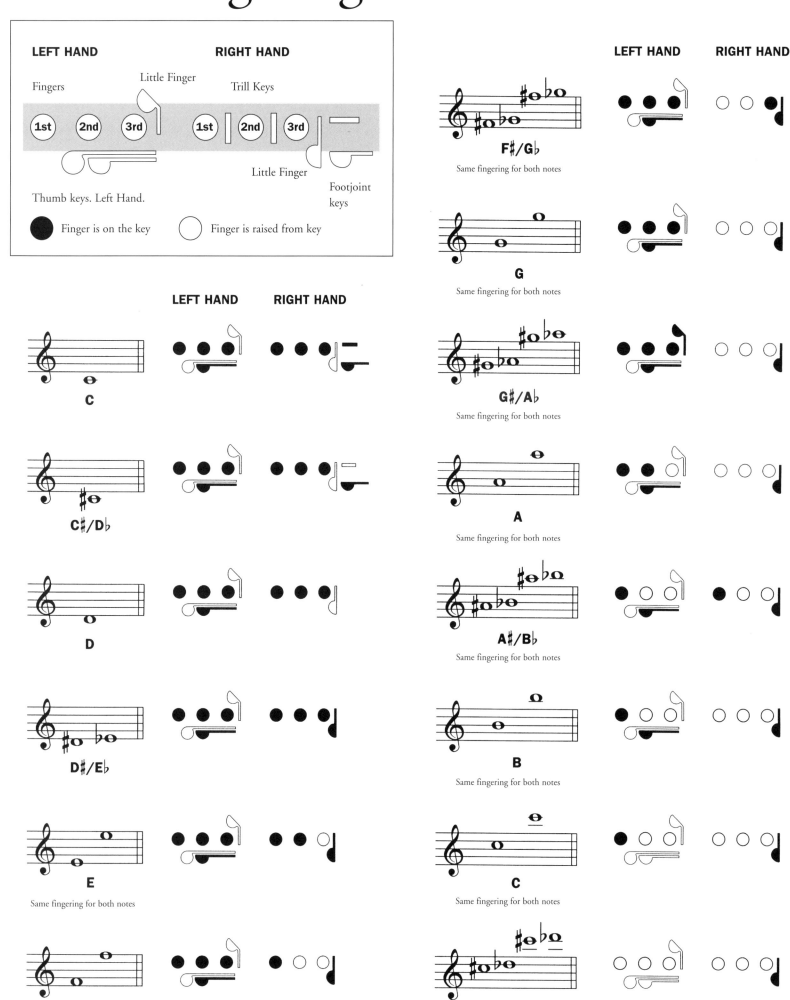

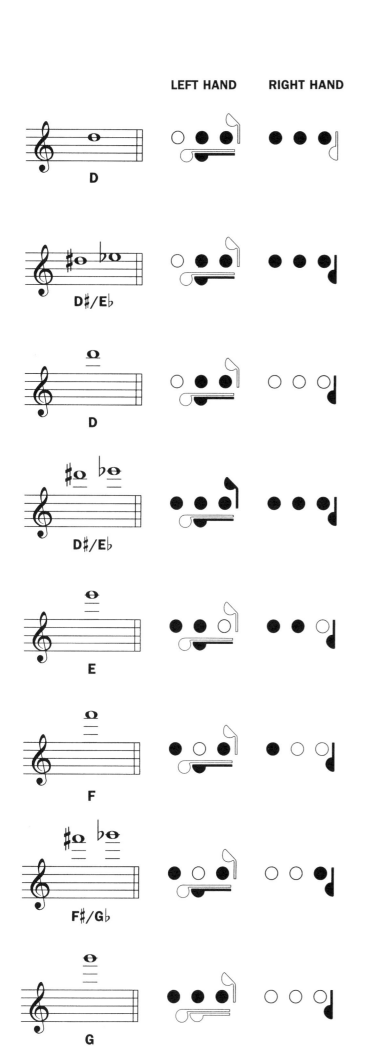

LEFT HAND | RIGHT HAND

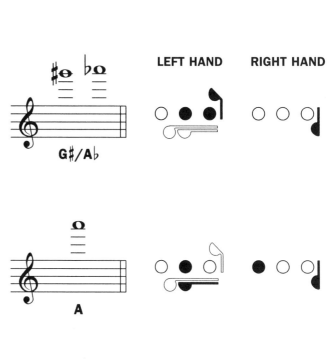

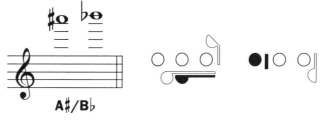

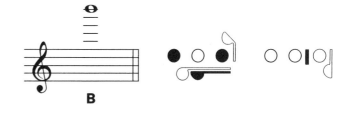

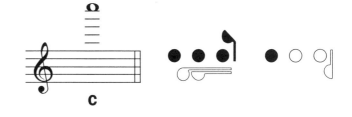

Defying Gravity
(from 'Wicked')

Words & Music by Stephen Schwartz

Expressively ♩ = 76

Good Morning Baltimore
(from 'Hairspray')

Words & Music by Marc Shaiman & Scott Wittman

Brightly, with a bounce ♩ = 132

molto rit.

Honey, Honey
(from 'Mamma Mia!')

Words & Music by Benny Andersson, Stig Anderson & Björn Ulvaeus

The Letter
(from 'Billy Elliot: The Musical')

Words by Lee Hall & Music by Elton John

Tenderly ♩ = 75

Love Never Dies

(from 'Love Never Dies')

Music by Andrew Lloyd Webber

Expressively ♩ = 129

(strings cue)

Più mosso ♩ = 80

p

mf espressivo

molto rit.   **A tempo** ♩ = 130

p   *mp*

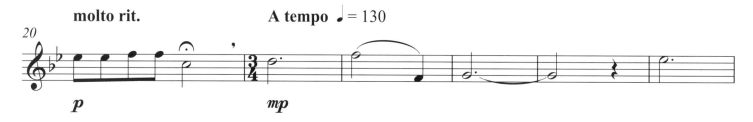

poco cresc.

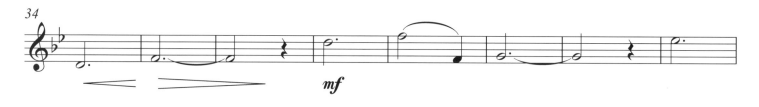

mf

Seasons Of Love
(from 'Rent')

Words & Music by Jonathan Larson

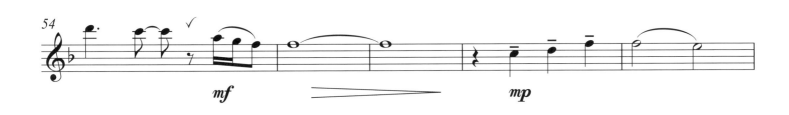

Suddenly Seymour
(from 'Little Shop Of Horrors')

Words by Howard Ashman
Music by Alan Menken

Expressively ♩ = 92

(piano cue)

A little faster ♩ = 102

mf ritmico

f

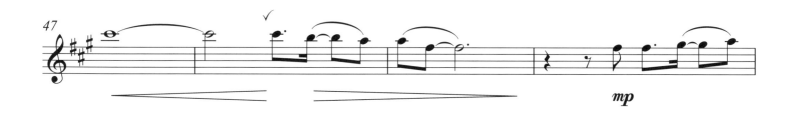

mp

Tell Me It's Not True
(from 'Blood Brothers')

Words & Music by Willy Russell

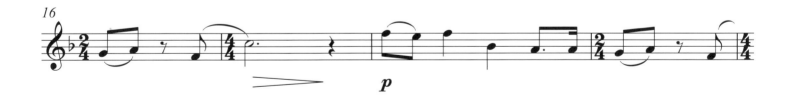

We Belong
(from 'Priscilla: Queen Of The Desert—The Musical')

Words & Music by Daniel Navarro & David Eric Lowen

Powerfully ♩ = 135

Gradual fade
to end

16

Working My Way Back To You
(from 'Jersey Boys')

Words & Music by Sandy Linzer & Denny Randell

legato e dolce

1 2 3 4 5 6 7 8 9

CD Track Listing

Full instrumental performances...

1. Tuning notes

2. Defying Gravity
   (Schwartz) Greydog Music

3. Good Morning Baltimore
   (Shaiman/Wittman) Songs of Pen UK

4. Honey, Honey
   (Andersson/Anderson/Ulvaeus) Bocu Music Limited

5. The Letter
   (Hall/John) Universal Music Publishing Limited

6. Love Never Dies
   (Webber) The Really Useful Group Limited

7. Seasons Of Love
   (Larson) Universal/MCA Music Limited

8. Suddenly Seymour
   (Ashman/Menken) Universal/MCA Music Limited/
   Warner/Chappell North America Limited

9. Tell Me It's Not True
   (Russell) W. R. Limited

10. We Belong
    (Navarro/Lowen) Screen Gems-EMI Music Limited

11. Working My Way Back To You
    (Linzer/Randell) Screen Gems-EMI Music Limited/EMI Music Publishing Limited

Backing tracks only...

12. Defying Gravity

13. Good Morning Baltimore

14. Honey, Honey

15. The Letter

16. Love Never Dies

17. Seasons Of Love

18. Suddenly Seymour

19. Tell Me It's Not True

20. We Belong

21. Working My Way Back To You

To remove your CD from the plastic sleeve, lift the small lip to break the perforations. Replace the disc after use for convenient storage